Don't Sit on My Lunch!

Don't Sit on My Lunch!

by ABBY KLEIN

illustrated by
JOHN MCKINLEY

SCHOLASTIC INC.
New York Toronto London Auckland Sydney
Mexico City New Delhi Hong Kong Buenos Aires

To J. K. —
The one who taught me a little bit
about hockey and a lot about love.
Love you forever.
—A. K.

No part of this publication may be reproduced in whole or in part,
stored in a retrieval system, or transmitted in any form or by any
means, electronic, mechanical, photocopying, recording, or
otherwise, without written permission of the publisher.
For information regarding permission, please write to: Permissions
Department, Scholastic Inc., 557 Broadway, New York, NY 10012.

This book is being published simultaneously in hardcover
by the Blue Sky Press.

ISBN 0-439-55602-3

Text copyright © 2005 by Abby Klein
Illustrations copyright © 2005 by John McKinley

Special thanks to Robert Martin Staenberg.

All rights reserved. Published by Scholastic Inc.
SCHOLASTIC and associated logos are trademarks
and/or registered trademarks of Scholastic Inc.

12 11 10 9 8 7 6 5 4 3 2 1   5 6 7 8 9 10/0

Printed in China   40

First Scholastic paperback printing, February 2005

CHAPTERS

I have a problem.

A really, really, big problem.

I want to try out for

the Pee Wee hockey team,

but so does Max, the biggest

bully in the whole first

grade, and there is only

one spot left.

Let me tell you about it.

CHAPTER 1

The Jersey

"Hey, where'd ya get that jersey?" Max asked Jessie, as we were walking to the cafeteria for lunch. "Is it your brother's?"

"Shhhh, Max, there is no talking in the hall," said our teacher, Mrs. Wushy. "Please zip your lips. You can chitchat when you are having lunch."

Max gave Mrs. Wushy a quick salute and then silently moved his thumb and pointer finger across his lips as if he were zipping them up.

When we arrived at the cafeteria, I sat down next to Jessie and my best friend, Robbie. I began unpacking my lunch: a peanut-butter-and-banana sandwich, a bag of cheese puffs, and a squeezable yogurt. I was just about to bite into my sandwich when Max elbowed me so hard I almost fell off the bench, and my sandwich dropped on the floor.

"Move over, wimp," he said, squeezing in between me and Jessie. "You are sitting in my spot."

When I bent down to get my sandwich, I bumped my head on the table on my way back up. "Ouch!" I complained, rubbing the top of my head.

"Oh, does the little baby need his mommy?" said Max.

"Are you OK, Freddy?" Jessie asked.

"Yeah, I'm OK. It just stings a little," I said, scooting over toward Robbie.

Jessie turned to Max. "You know, Freddy was sitting there."

"Not anymore he isn't. *I* am. Now where did you get that jersey? I want one."

"It *is* really cool, Jessie," I said.

Max whipped his head around and snapped, "Was I talking to you, pip-squeak?"

I shook my head.

"Boy, what a poop," Robbie whispered in my ear.

"What'd you say?" Max snarled.

"Oh, nothing," Robbie answered, as he turned to me and smiled.

"Well, I don't think you'll ever have one of these jerseys," Jessie said. "You can't buy it in the store. It's my team jersey."

"Your what?" Max asked, confused.

"My team jersey. My team is called the Hammerheads."

"No, really, where'd you get it?" Max asked, snickering.

"I told you," Jessie said, getting a little annoyed. "I play for the Hammerheads, and this is our team jersey."

"Wow! That's great!" I said. "I didn't know you played ice hockey."

"I didn't either," said the class priss, Chloe, wrinkling up her nose. "That's not very ladylike of you."

"Girls don't play hockey," said Max.

"Says who?" Jessie demanded, glaring at Max. She was starting to get really irritated, and I thought any minute she might haul off and punch Max right in the nose. She was probably the only one in the whole

13

class brave enough to take on Max Sellars, the biggest bully in all of first grade.

"I've never met a girl who plays hockey."

"Well, now you have," Jessie said, smiling.

"What happens if the puck hits you in the face?" Chloe asked with a sick look. "You could be scarred for life!"

"All the good hockey players have scars."

"That's terrible," said Chloe. "I would never want to do anything that might scar my beautiful face. That's why I do ballet."

"How did you get on the team?" I asked.

"I was taking skating lessons down at the rink, and one of the coaches suggested

I try out for the team. It looked like fun, so I tried out, and I made it."

"You must be really good."

"Naw," Jessie said, blushing. "Hey, why don't you try out, Freddy? You like to ice-skate, and our team still needs one more player for this season."

"Maybe *I'll* try out," Max piped up. "Skating as fast as you can and smashing people into the boards. Sounds like a lot of fun to me!"

"But there's only one spot left, Max," Jessie said, "and I think Freddy is going to take it. He can beat you any day."

"That little baby?" Max said, pointing to me and laughing. "I'm way better than he is. He'll never beat me."

"We'll see about that," Jessie said, winking at me. "Tryouts are this coming Saturday,

and then we'll really see who the best player is. Right, Freddy?"

"Right," I said, smiling weakly.

"What are you doing? Have you lost your mind?" Robbie whispered in my ear. "You don't know how to play hockey."

"I know," I whispered back. "What do I do now? I'm in big trouble."

CHAPTER 2

Convincing Mom

I definitely had my work cut out for me. First, I was going to have to convince my mom to let me play. And *that* was not going to be easy. She doesn't like sports too much. She thinks hockey and football are very dangerous. Her idea of a good sport is chess.

My dad, on the other hand, is really into sports. He is always trying to get me to join a team. If I could get him excited about hockey, then maybe he could convince my mom to let me play.

"Guess what I heard at school today?" I said at dinner.

"That you're going to flunk first grade?" my big sister Suzie said.

"Oh, that's so funny I forgot to laugh," I said, glaring at her. "No, I heard that the Pee Wee hockey league is going to have tryouts on Saturday."

"Oh, really?" my dad said, looking up from his plate.

Good. I had his attention. "Yeah, and the Hammerheads need one more player."

"Don't worry," my mom said. "They'll find somebody good."

Boy, she wasn't going to make this easy. "Uh, no . . . I . . . uh . . . I . . . thought . . . you know how Dad's always telling me to join a team. . . . I thought . . . maybe I . . . would try out."

"HOCKEY?!!" my mom screamed, almost choking on her broccoli. "Are you crazy? There is no way any child of mine is going to play that sport."

Great. This wasn't going exactly as I had planned.

"You! Oh, that's hilarious," Suzie said, laughing. "You're such a wimp. The team isn't called the Hammerheads for nothing. You know you can really get nailed out there on the ice!"

"Shut up, Brat!" I yelled back. "Dad, can you help me out here?"

"First of all, honey," my dad said to my

mom, "please calm down. We can't discuss this if you're hysterical."

"DISCUSS THIS!" my mom shouted. "THERE IS NOTHING TO DISCUSS!"

"Oh, come on now, Debbie," my dad continued. "Freddy might actually have a good idea here."

That's it, Dad. Keep going.

"A good idea! Now *you've* gone crazy. Freddy is way too little to play such a rough sport. He'll break his cute little nose."

"This isn't the NHL, honey. It's Pee Wee hockey. How rough can it be? I know for a fact that there's no checking at this age."

"What are you talking about?"

"No checking means they're not allowed to hit each other."

"Great, so another kid won't break

his nose, but a flying puck might," my mom said.

"That might be an improvement on his face," Suzie said, chuckling.

I glared at her. My dad ignored her. "The kids have to wear a full face mask. They are totally protected."

Wow! This was great. I didn't have to say a word. My dad was doing just fine all on his own.

"I still don't think it's a good idea."

"I do," my dad said. "It's good exercise, and it will help strengthen his hand-eye coordination in preparation for those piano lessons you want him to take."

You go, Dad. Now he was really on a roll. That piano-lesson comment was pure genius, I tell you!

"I think it would be good for Freddy to be on a team and learn a little something about sportsmanship."

"Yeah, considering he's such a bad loser," Suzie said.

"I am not!" I shouted back.

"Yes you are!"

"No I'm not!"

"Oh yes you are!"

"ENOUGH, YOU TWO!" my dad barked. Then he turned to my mom. "So, come on, Deb. What do you think?"

"Well . . . " my mom started.

She was almost there. I could feel it. *Just bring it on home, Dad.*

"Um, excuse me. Are you kidding me?" Suzie interrupted again. "You're really going to let that little weakling play hockey? The equipment weighs more than he does."

Oh no! Oh no! My dumb sister was about to spoil everything.

"Suzie, stay out of this," my dad said, pointing his finger at her. "This is none of your business." He turned back to my mom. "Debbie, I think we should at least let him try out. If he makes the team, then you can make your final decision."

"I just don't know, Daniel," she said, shaking her head.

"Pleeeease, Mom," I begged. "Pretty please with a cherry on top."

"Oh, all right. You can try out. But I'm not making any promises."

I ran over to her and threw my arms around her neck. "You're the best mom in the whole world! Thank you! Thank you! Thank you!"

CHAPTER 3

K-I-S-S-I-N-G

Later that night, I was watching my favorite cartoon, *Commander Upchuck*, when the phone rang.

"Freddy!" my mom called from the kitchen. "It's for you!"

"Who is it?" I yelled back.

"I don't know! It's a girl."

I felt my cheeks get hot. My stomach did a flip. Did she have to yell that so that everyone, including my busybody sister, could hear?

"Freddy's got a girlfriend! Freddy's got a girlfriend!" Suzie sang out, gleefully.

"I do not!" I snapped back.

"Freddy!" my mom called again. "Pick up the phone!"

"OK, Mom, I got it! Hello?"

"Hi, Freddy," said the voice on the other end. It was Jessie.

"Could you hang on a minute?" I could tell my mom hadn't hung up yet. I yelled to her, "OK, Mom, I've got it. You can hang up now!" I heard the phone click. Then I carried the phone into the other room to get away from my nosy sister.

"Hey, Jessie," I said.

"Oooohhh, Jessie," my sister cooed. I

didn't realize that she had followed me into the other room.

"Go away!" I yelled.

"Suuuzie!" my dad called. "Come back in here and leave him alone, or you're going to be in big trouble."

She marched out in a huff, and I stuck my tongue out after her. "Hey, Jessie," I said again. "What's up?"

"Hey, Freddy," she said. "Do you want to come over after school tomorrow and practice some hockey?"

"Where?"

"Right next to my apartment there's an empty parking lot. It's a great place to skate. I know it's not ice, but we can practice on our Rollerblades anyway."

"Uh, sure. Let me just ask my mom." I walked into the kitchen. "Mom, can I go to Jessie's after school tomorrow? We have to work on a special project."

"I don't see why not. Jessie is a great person to do a project with. She's such a good student. You can ride the bus home with her, and then I'll pick you up when you're done working."

"Thanks, Mom!" I carried the phone

into the other room again. "Jessie, my mom says I can go."

"Great! Don't forget your skates."

"I won't. See you tomorrow!"

"Yeah, see you tomorrow!"

I hung up the phone and turned to go back to the TV room. My sister had snuck into the living room and was staring at me. "Ahhhh!" I said. "You scared the bejeebees out of me. What does someone have to do to get a little privacy around here?"

Just then my sister started singing really loudly, "Freddy and Jessie, sitting in a tree. K-I-S-S-I-N-G."

I could feel my face getting really hot. I'm sure my cheeks were turning as red as a tomato.

"First comes love, then comes marriage,

then comes a baby in a baby carriage,"
Suzie continued, dancing around me.

I raised my fist and lunged toward her.
"Why you little . . . I'm going to . . . "

Just as I was about to punch her right in
the nose, my dad came in and grabbed me.
"All right, Freddy, calm down. What's
going on in here?"

"Let me at her! Let me at her!" I said, punching the air and trying to break free of my dad's grip.

"Did you know that Freddy has a girl-friend?" Suzie asked, smirking.

"I DO NOT!" I screamed. "I'M JUST GOING OVER TO JESSIE'S TO WORK ON A SPECIAL PROJECT!"

"Oh, a special project," said Suzie. "OK, if that's what you want to call it."

"Suzie," my dad demanded, "go to your room right now!"

"But, Dad," she protested.

"No arguing with the referee. You have a ten-minute misconduct penalty, young lady. Now, go!"

She started to go and then turned back. "Toodles, Loverboy," she said, blowing a kiss in my direction.

I lunged toward the door, but my dad held me tight. "Ignore her," my dad said. "She's just trying to make you crazy. And she seems to be doing a pretty good job."

I started to laugh. "Dad, I liked that little referee thing you did. Can we send her to the penalty box more often?"

"Hey, I have an idea, Freddy. Let's you and I go to a hockey game sometime."

"That sounds great, Dad. I can't wait. When can we go?"

"I'll talk to your mom. All right, champ? Now, go get ready for bed. I'll be up in a minute. And no more face-offs with your sister."

"Thanks, Dad. You're the best!"

CHAPTER 4

Ten-Minute Misconduct

The next day in the cafeteria, Max elbowed his way in between me and Jessie again, and this time I couldn't get my lunch out of the way fast enough.

"Hey, watch it!" I said. "Your big, fat butt is squishing my baloney sandwich!"

"No, you watch it, Shrimp," he snapped. Then he bounced up and down on my lunch a few more times before handing it back to me. "I think this belongs to you."

"Well, that wasn't very nice," Chloe said. "Your mother needs to teach you some manners, Max."

"And your mother needs to teach you to stop talking so much," Max replied.

I slowly peeked in my lunch bag. My baloney sandwich was a gushy mess, my chocolate-chip cookies were all crumbs, and my cherry tomatoes now looked more like ketchup. Yuck!

"What's it look like?" Robbie asked.

"Like a dog threw up," I said.

"Here. I can share my sandwich with you," he said, handing me half of his turkey and swiss.

"Thanks," I said. Turkey isn't exactly my

favorite, but I couldn't really be picky at a time like this.

Max turned to Jessie. "When did you say those hockey tryouts were?"

"Why do you care?" she asked.

"Because I'm going to try out."

I almost choked on my sandwich. Actually, Robbie's sandwich.

"You?" Jessie said, pointing at Max and laughing. "*You're* going to try out?"

"Yeah, me. What's so funny about me playing hockey?"

"You may be a good skater, but hockey is a *team* sport. You have to work together with other people to score goals. You can't just hog the puck."

"That's why I like to do ballet," Chloe interrupted. "I don't have to worry about anybody but myself. I get to be the star."

"You can't always be the star in hockey," Jessie continued. "You depend on your teammates a lot."

"Then that is definitely not the sport for me," Chloe said, pointing a red-painted fingernail at herself. "Besides, I like things that are more elegant and sophisticated. Hockey is so . . . so . . . *piggish*."

"And you wouldn't want to chip your nail polish," Jessie said, smiling.

"Well, that's true, too. A good manicure costs fifteen dollars, you know."

"Shut up already about your nails," said Max. "No one cares."

"You're not allowed to say 'shut up,'" Chloe whined.

"Oh yeah? You want to do something about it?" Max asked, leaning over the table and shaking a fist in her face.

Chloe shook her head and went back to eating her sushi.

"I didn't think so." He turned back to Jessie. "I know how to play on a team," Max said. "I played on the after-school basketball team."

"And you hogged the ball the whole time," Jessie said. "You never passed the ball to your teammates. Hockey is all about passing the puck around. In fact, you not only get points for making a goal, you also get a point for making an assist."

"What's that?" Max asked.

"If you pass the puck to someone, and that person makes a goal, then you get a point for an assist. You get points for helping someone else."

"The only person Max helps is himself," Chloe said, waving a chopstick in the air.

The next thing she knew, Max grabbed the chopstick and broke it in half.

"Now how am I going to finish my sushi with only one chopstick?" Chloe sniffled. "You're so mean. I'm telling on you. Miss Becky!" she called.

Miss Becky, the lunch helper, came over. "Yes, Chloe? Is something wrong?"

"First Max sat on Freddy's lunch. Then he told me to shut up, and now he broke my chopstick. I think he should have to go eat at the time-out table."

"Come on. Let's go, Max," Miss Becky said, marching him to the time-out table.

"Hey, Max, I know one thing in hockey you would be really good at," Jessie called after him.

"Oh yeah? What's that?"

"Sitting in the penalty box," Jessie said, laughing. "You're already an all-star!"

CHAPTER 5

Goals and Guacamole

That afternoon, when the bus stopped in front of Jessie's apartment, we both started to get off.

"Hey, where are you going? This isn't your stop," Robbie called, as Jessie and I made our way down the aisle.

Rats. I was hoping to get off before anyone realized I was going to a girl's house. "I . . . uh . . . I gotta get off here," I yelled back, as I jumped down the last few steps of the bus.

"Huh?" Robbie called, but I was already halfway to the front door of the apartment building, and the bus started to pull away.

"Well, here we are," Jessie said. "Let's go upstairs and put our backpacks down and have a snack. Then we can go practice in that parking lot over there," she said, pointing to a big, empty lot right next to her building.

We climbed the stairs to her apartment, and she rang the bell. Her grandma answered and let us in. *"Hola, abuela. ¿Cómo estás?"*

"Bien, gracias."

"Aquí está mi amigo, Freddy."

I waved. *"Hola."*

"My grandma lives with me and my

46

mom. She takes care of me after school when my mom is at work."

"You're lucky. I don't get to see my grandparents every day," I said.

"Yeah, I like having her around. And she's a great cook. Do you want to try one of her world-famous tamales for a snack?"

"What's a tamale?"

"What's a *tamale*? You mean you've never tasted a tamale before?" Jessie said, with her mouth hanging open.

"Nope."

"Then you're in for a treat. Follow me."

We went into the kitchen, and her grandma pulled a plate of tamales out of the fridge and warmed them up in the microwave. Then she put them on the table and said, "*Coman, coman.*"

"That means eat," Jessie said.

"How do you eat it?" I asked, staring at the plate in front of me.

"Watch. First, you peel off the corn husk it's wrapped in. Then you cut it up, dip it in guacamole, and pop it in your mouth like this."

I'm really a macaroni-and-cheese kind

of guy, but I didn't want to make Jessie or her grandma feel bad, so I decided to try it. "Wow! This is yummy!" I said, with a mouth full of tamale.

"I know! I told you they were world famous," Jessie said, smiling.

Between the two of us, we finished the whole plate of tamales. "I'm stuffed," I said, patting my stomach.

"Not too stuffed to play, I hope," said Jessie. "Come on. Let's go get our skates."

We thanked her grandma, grabbed our skates, helmets, sticks, and a puck, and headed back downstairs. When we got outside, we put on our helmets and skates, and Jessie said, "Race ya to that wall over there."

I skated as fast as I could, but she beat me. "Wow! You're really fast!" I said.

"You have to skate fast to play hockey." Jessie took off across the parking lot and then started back toward me. As she got close, I covered my eyes and screamed, "AHHHHH!" I thought for sure she was about to crash into me, but she stopped about two inches in front of my nose. I opened one eye and peeked at her.

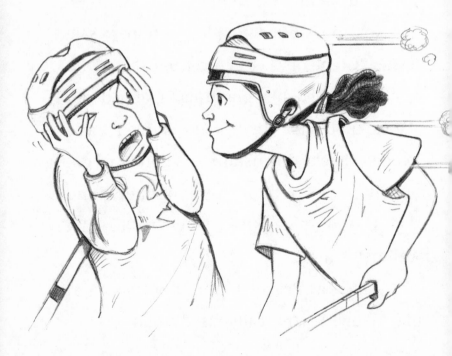

Jessie laughed. "You're such a fraidy cat, Freddy. If you're going to play hockey, you can't close your eyes when people skate toward you."

"Then maybe hockey just isn't the right sport for me."

"What? You're going to give up just like that? Don't be such a wimp. Max will tease you about it for the rest of your life. Besides, I want *you* on my team, not Max."

"Really?"

"Yeah. I think it would be fun to be teammates. So what do you say?"

"Yeah. I think that would be fun, too," I said, smiling.

"OK, so let's get to work. First, let me show you how to hold the stick the right way. Are you right-handed or left-handed?"

"Right-handed."

"Then you put your right hand down low on the stick and your left hand up high. Like this."

"Is this right?" I asked.

"Yeah, just like that. Now, you don't want to push the puck."

"You don't?"

"No. You want to flick your wrist. That will make the puck go farther and faster. Watch me." Jessie flicked her wrist, and the puck went sailing down the parking lot.

"Wow! That was amazing," I said.

Jessie brought the puck back and dropped it on the ground. "Now you try it."

I flicked my wrist but missed the puck altogether. Jessie started giggling.

"Thanks a lot," I said.

"I'm sorry, Freddy, but that was really funny. Why don't you try again?"

"You promise you won't laugh?"

"I promise."

"Cross your heart?"

"Cross my heart," Jessie said, making a big X on her chest.

I flicked my wrist again, and this time, to my surprise, the puck flew across the lot.

"Holy cow!" Jessie said. "That was awesome! Look how far it went, Freddy." Jessie was a really good teacher. She taught me how to shoot, pass, and make a goal.

When it started getting dark, Jessie said, "I think we'd better go in, but if you come back again, I can teach you more about the rules and the different positions."

"Cool," I said. "This was really fun. Thanks, Jessie."

"No problem, Freddy. I had fun, too. Do you want to borrow one of my sticks, so you can practice at home?"

"Yeah. That'd be great! You sure you don't mind?"

"Nope. What are friends for?"

I smiled. With Jessie's help, maybe I could beat Max after all.

CHAPTER 6

A Flick
of the Wrist

That night at dinner, I was so excited that I couldn't stop thinking about hockey. "Jessie's a really good teacher, Dad. She taught me a lot today."

"Wow! That's great," my dad said. "Like what?"

"Well, she taught me how to shoot the puck. She said you have to flick your wrist," I said, picking up my knife to demonstrate. "Like this. He shoots . . . " I flicked my wrist, and a big lump of mashed potatoes went sailing across the table and splatted right in Suzie's face.

"He scores!"

"Eeewwwww!" she screamed, as she wiped potato out of her eye. "You little brat! I'm going to get you for this!" she said, lunging across the table to grab my shirt. A large bowl of peas fell off the table and spilled all over the floor.

"Let's all calm down," my mom said, scrambling to pick up the peas. "Just look at this mess!"

"CALM DOWN! CALM DOWN!" Suzie screamed. "That's easy for you to say. You don't have mashed potato in your eye and up your nose!"

"Let me help you wipe it off," my dad

said. "Freddy, how many times have I told you not to play with your food?"

"I wasn't playing. I was just trying to show you how Jessie taught me to flick my wrist."

"Well, no more demonstrations," my dad said. "Suzie, why don't you go wash the

potato off your face? Freddy, I think you should say you're sorry to your sister and help your mom pick up the peas."

"But I didn't spill the peas. Suzie did."

"Fre-ddy," my dad said. "Don't argue with me here, or you won't be playing hockey at all."

"But, Dad."

"No 'buts.' We have to help your mother—*now*."

I bent down to help. "You know, Mom, if we had a dog, we wouldn't have to be cleaning this up right now. A dog is like a vacuum cleaner. If anything spills on the floor, the dog licks it right up."

"How many times do I have to tell you we're not getting a dog? They're dirty, and smelly, and they shed. I'll clean my own floors, thank you very much."

I shrugged. Oh well. It was worth a try.

My dad leaned over and whispered in my ear, "She's letting you try out for hockey. You're lucky you got that."

Just then Suzie came back from washing her face. She stood over me with her hands on her hips and cleared her throat, "Uhhh-hmmmm."

"Yeah, what?" I asked, looking up at her.

"I'm waiting," she said.

"Waiting for what?"

"For an apology."

Oh brother. "I'm sorry, you little baby."

"Dad!" Suzie whined. "Did you hear that?"

"Fre-ddy," my dad said. "I want you to say you're sorry without calling your sister any names."

"Fine. I'm sorry."

"You didn't mean it," Suzie said. "You have to say it again."

"What?!"

"Say it again."

"No way."

"All right. Enough, you two," my dad said. "Suzie, Freddy already said he was sorry. Now, can we finish what's left of our dinner in peace?"

"Yes, that would be nice," my mom said, pulling in her chair. "Kids, sit down.

And no more hockey demonstrations while we are eating, please."

When things calmed down again, Suzie said, "Hey, I thought you were going over to Jessie's to work on some special project for school, not play hockey."

Oops. In all my excitement, I had let it slip that Jessie was teaching me hockey. "Yeah . . . well . . . we . . . umm . . . "

"So Jessie plays hockey," my mom said, smiling. "Now I get it."

"Get what?"

"Why you want to play hockey so badly."

She was not making any sense. "I already told you why. Because it's a really fun sport."

"Right, right," she said, winking at my dad.

I hate when they do that. It's like a secret grown-up code. "Will you stop smiling and winking?" I said.

"But I think it's sweet," my mom told me.

"What's sweet?" I yelled. "I have no idea what you are talking about! You're making me crazy!"

"I think it's cute that you have a little girlfriend."

"I DO NOT HAVE A GIRLFRIEND! HOW MANY TIMES DO I HAVE TO TELL YOU PEOPLE THAT?"

Suzie started singing that stupid song again: "Freddy and Jessie sitting in a tree. K-I-S-S-I-N-G."

"LEAVE ME ALONE!" I screamed, as I tried to hold back my tears.

"Oh, Freddy, I'm sorry," my mom said.

"I didn't mean to get you so upset. Come here. Let me give you a hug."

I walked over and sat down in my mom's lap. She put her arms around me and gave me a big squeeze.

"Jessie is just helping me learn how

to play hockey," I said, sniffling. "I really, really, really want to beat Max Sellars and get the last spot on the team."

"And you will, Mouse," my dad said.

"Uh, Dad?" I said, wiping my nose on my sleeve.

"Yeah?"

"Do you think maybe you could call me something else? Mouse doesn't really sound like a hockey player's name."

"What do you mean? Mouse is a great name. Mice are quick, they move easily in and out of tight spots, and they almost never get caught. Just like a good hockey player."

"Hey, yeah. You're right. Just call me Freddy, the Mouse, Thresher," I said. "I'll move so fast that no one will be able to catch me. Not even Max Sellars."

CHAPTER 7

The Bet

The day before tryouts, Max was bragging to everyone at recess about how he was going to kick my butt. "Freddy? That little wimp," he said, snickering. "There's no way he's going to beat me. I could skate better than him with my eyes closed."

"Oh yeah? You wanna bet?" Jessie said.

"What?" Max asked, whipping his head around to stare Jessie right in the eyes. "Did you say something?"

"Yeah. I said, do you want to bet? I'll bet

you your snack for one whole week that Freddy makes the team, and you don't."

"You feeling OK?" Max asked, putting his palm on Jessie's forehead. "I think you've lost your marbles."

"Get your hands off me!" Jessie said, swiping Max's hand away. "I'm fine.

What's wrong? Are you afraid to bet because you know you're gonna lose?"

"Lose? I never lose."

"That's because you're a big cheater," Chloe said, interrupting.

Max turned and stuck his finger in her face. "Was I talking to you?"

"Well, no, but . . . "

"Then be quiet," Max barked.

"Ooohhh, you're so mean," Chloe said. "I don't know why you have to be such a big bully, Max Sellars."

"And I don't know why you have to be so annoying."

"You are so rude!" Chloe said, pouting and putting her hands on her hips. "My mother says I should just ignore you, so that's what I'm going to do." Then she put her fingers in her ears.

"Whatever, you cuckoo bird," Max said.

"I can't hear you," Chloe said, and she walked away, humming.

"I know Freddy's going to beat you tomorrow," Jessie said, "because I've been helping him practice all week."

"Oh *really*?" Max said, grinning. He turned to me. "So Jessie's been teaching you how to play hockey. I can't believe you've been getting help from a girl," Max said, laughing.

I was so embarrassed, I wished someone could make me disappear.

"And what's wrong with that?" Jessie asked, sticking her nose in Max's face.

"Everyone knows girls don't know as much about sports as boys do," Max said.

"Says who?" Jessie demanded.

Hey, if Jessie could stand up to Max Sellars, then maybe I could, too. "Yeah," I piped up. "Jessie just happens to be the best hockey player I've ever seen, boy or girl." Before I could even think about what I was saying, I said, "And you know what? Snack for a whole week isn't enough. I'll bet you your snack for the whole week and your dessert at lunch, too."

Robbie grabbed me by the arm and whispered in my ear, "What are you doing? Are you crazy? This is Max Sellars we're talking about here. I am your best friend. I can't let you do this."

"Thanks, but I know what I'm doing."

"Stop whispering, you two. Come on, Shrimp. Do we have a bet or not?"

I looked over at Jessie. She was nodding and smiling at me. "Go for it," she mouthed.

"You're on!" I said, sticking out my hand to shake Max's. "Snack and dessert for a whole week."

"Oh, I can just taste your mom's home-made chocolate-chip cookies now," Max said, as he shook my hand.

"In your dreams, Max. In your dreams."

CHAPTER 8

My Lucky Underwear

The morning of the tryouts I was going crazy because I couldn't find my lucky underwear. I had my lucky shark tooth, but I would never beat Max Sellars if I didn't have on my underwear with the great white sharks on it. I had already dumped everything out of my underwear drawer twice, and I'd tossed half the junk out of my closet without any luck. I decided to check the dirty clothes hamper in the bathroom. Of course, the bathroom door was locked because Suzie was in there all morning, as usual.

"Hey, let me in!" I said, pounding on the door.

"Go away, Poophead," Suzie called back.

"Suzie, it's an emergency. Let me in."

"Go use Mom and Dad's bathroom if you have to pee so badly."

"No, it's not that kind of emergency. I'm looking for something. Come on, Suzie. Open up."

"Well, you'd better make it quick," Suzie said, opening the door.

"Thanks," I said, pushing my way in.

"What are you looking for anyway?"

"My great white underwear," I said, tossing the dirty clothes all over the floor.

"Why?"

"Because it's my lucky underwear."

"You are crazy, you know that," Suzie said. "I can't believe I'm related to you."

"Oh, here they are," I said, reaching way down to the bottom of the hamper. I pulled them out and kissed them.

"Eeewww! Gross! You just kissed your dirty underpants."

I pulled off my pajama bottoms and started to put the underwear on.

"Uh, Freddy, what are you doing?"

"I told you. I'm putting on my lucky underwear for the tryouts." I said, pulling them up around my waist.

"But they're dirty. They were in the dirty clothes hamper."

"So?"

"So, you know Mom doesn't let us wear underwear for more than one day."

"But I *have* to wear this underwear today. If I don't, there's no way I can beat Max."

"But Mom won't let you."

"The only way she'll know is if you tell her. Please don't tell her."

"What's in it for me?" Suzie asked.

"I'll make your bed for a week."

"Wow! You must really want to wear that underwear," said Suzie. "Fine. It's a deal," she said, as we locked pinkies. "Pinkie swear?" she said.

"Pinkie swear," I said.

"Hey, Freddy, wait!" Suzie said, as I was walking out of the bathroom. She ran into her bedroom and came back with a penny. "Here. This is my good-luck penny. Put it in your skate today, and then you'll beat Max for sure."

"Thanks," I said, taking the penny from her. "You're the best sister in the world."

"I know," she said, smiling.

CHAPTER 9

He Shoots . . .

When we got to the tryouts, I was so nervous I thought I was going to throw up. I wasn't so sure that the underwear, the penny, and my lucky shark tooth would be enough to beat Max Sellars. After all, he was the biggest bully in the whole first grade.

The coach blew his whistle. "OK, everybody, listen up. If you are here for the tryouts, come line up on the blue line."

"Good luck, honey," my mom said, giving me a hug.

"Go get 'em, Mouse," said my dad.

I took a deep breath, stepped onto the ice, and skated over to the blue line.

"All right. We're going to do a couple of drills, and then we are going to have a little scrimmage," said the coach.

He took notes while we skated forward and backward, took shots on goal, and did some stick-handling around cones.

So far, so good, I thought, thanks to my shark tooth, Suzie's penny, and my lucky underwear.

"Now I'm going to divide you up into two teams, and we're going to play a game. You, you, and you," he said, pointing to three boys to my left, "go put on the red jerseys. And you, you, and you," he said, pointing to me, Max, and another kid, "go put on the blue jerseys."

Max turned and gave me the evil eye.

Oh great. It looked like my luck had just run out.

We all put on our jerseys. Then the coach blew the whistle, dropped the puck, and the game began.

We skated back and forth. They took shots. We took some shots. I made a few good passes.

I looked over to the bench and saw Jessie smiling. She gave me a thumbs-up.

Later on in the game, a player from the other team came skating toward me so fast that when I tried to move out of the way, I tripped over my own feet and fell to the ice. Because of my mistake, the other team went on to score a goal.

"Thanks a lot, loser," Max growled.

This time when I looked up at the bench, Jessie wasn't smiling anymore.

With one minute left, the score was tied two–two. A player from the red team made a shot on goal, but the goalie blocked it, and the puck bounced to the corner. I skated after it, but Max cut in front of me, and he

got to the puck first. He started to skate down the ice, heading toward the goal.

I remembered that Jessie had told me this: If your teammate is skating down the ice toward the goal, you should skate down there, too, to pick up any rebounds.

I started to skate toward the goal and glanced up at the clock. There were only eleven seconds left.

As Max got close to the goal, two of the boys from the red team surrounded him. There was no way he was going to be able to shoot. Max looked up and saw me.

Before I knew it, Max made a great pass
across the ice, right onto my stick. I flicked
my wrist, just like Jessie had told me, and
the puck went sailing toward the goal. I
watched as it flipped, end over end, past
the goalie's outstretched glove, and into the
back of the net.

I couldn't believe it. *I* had made the winning goal with the help of Max Sellars!

The next thing I knew, Max had skated over to me and was hugging me, actually crushing me, and yelling, "We did it! We did it! We did it!"

Somebody pinch me. I must have been

dreaming. Was Max Sellars really saying something nice to me?

I should've known better. In the next breath, Max said, "Remember, only one of us can make the team, and it looks like it's going to be me."

"What makes you so sure?" I asked.

"I was the best skater out there."

"Don't be so sure," Jessie said. She had skated out to join us on the ice. "I think Freddy was awesome," she said, giving me a hug. I felt my cheeks get hot.

"Well, it doesn't matter what you think," said Max. "You're not the one who's deciding."

Just then the coach blew his whistle and asked everyone to line up.

"You all did a great job today. I wish I could take all of you, but I can't. I do have some good news, though. Originally, I had room for only one new member of the team, but one of our players had to drop out yesterday, so I have room for two of you."

My heart was beating so fast I thought it was going to pop out of my chest.

"I have made my decision, and I've picked Max Sellars and Freddy Thresher."

My mouth dropped open. I couldn't believe it. *I* had made the team. Freddy Thresher was now a member of the Hammerheads. My dad was jumping up and down. Jessie was smiling and holding my hand. This was the happiest day of my life.

And then Max slapped me on the back and said, "Hey, looks like you and I are on the same team."

DEAR READER,

I have been teaching children for fifteen years, so I know a lot about bullies. Every year there is a new bully in first grade. Bullies can be very cruel, and they make you feel scared and afraid to tell anyone about what they are doing.

When I was in first grade, I was very small. Every day at lunch, a boy who was much bigger than me used to take my dessert. I didn't want him to, but I thought if I told anyone, he would beat me up. Finally, I got up enough courage to tell my mom and dad. Then they told the principal, and the boy was punished. He also never bothered me again.

Bullies pick on people they think won't speak up or tell on them. So speak up for yourself and your friends and put bullies in their place! If you'd like to tell me about the biggest bully in your school, just write to me at:

Ready, Freddy! Fun Stuff
c/o Scholastic Inc.
P. O. Box 711
New York, NY 10013-0711

I hope you have as much fun reading *Don't Sit on My Lunch!* as I had writing it.

HAPPY READING!

Abby Klein

Freddy's Fun Pages

FREDDY'S SHARK JOURNAL

WHAT DO SHARKS EAT FOR LUNCH?

All sharks are carnivores.

Different species of sharks eat different kinds of food.

The big whale shark feeds on teeny, tiny creatures called plankton.

Tiger sharks eat very large animals like sea lions.

Some sharks even eat other sharks!

Most sharks do not need to eat every day, but I do!

JESSIE'S GRANDMA'S FIESTA NACHOS

Try making these delicious nachos. They are one of Jessie's favorite after-school snacks.

YOU WILL NEED:

tortilla chips
grated cheddar cheese
grated jack cheese

1. Spread the tortilla chips out on a microwave-safe plate.

2. Sprinkle the jack and cheddar cheese over the chips. Make sure to cover all the chips with cheese.

3. Have your mom or dad cook the nachos in the microwave on High for 30 seconds, or until the cheese is melted.

4. Let stand for five minutes before eating. They will be very hot.

5. Eat plain or add salsa, sour cream, and guacamole.

ENJOY!

A VERY SILLY STORY
by Freddy Thresher

Help Freddy write a silly story by filling in the blanks
on the next three pages. The description under each
blank tells you what kind of word to use. Don't read
the story until you have filled in all the blanks!

HELPFUL HINTS:

A **verb** is an action word (such as run, jump, or hide).
An **adjective** describes a person, place, or thing
(such as smelly, loud, or blue).

It was lunchtime, and _____ and I

a friend

were sitting together in the _____

an adjective

cafeteria. I had the _____ lunch

an adjective ending in –est

ever: a _____ _____ sandwich

a color   your favorite food

topped with _____ _____ slices.

a flavor   a vegetable

_____ had a really _____ lunch,
   The same friend   an adjective

too: a bowl of _____ _____
            an adjective   something you drink

and some _____ crackers.
         an adjective

"My _____ packed a _____ snack
     a parent   an adjective

for me today," I said. "See? It's _____
                          your favorite color

and _____ gummi _____!"
  your least favorite color   your favorite animals

"Yucky! They taste just like a _____
                            an adjective

_____!"
  a noun

"Well, I really _____ them," I said.
               a verb

"I _____ _____ every day."
   a verb   a number

"Hey, let me show you something even

_____," said _____.
 an adjective ending in –er   the same friend

"Chocolate-covered _____.
                          your least favorite fruits

Want to try one?"

     We were just about to start _____
                                        a verb ending in –ing

when _____ sat down across from
          a second friend

us and said, "Who wants to trade for some

_____ _____ salad
     an adjective   a kind of food

and a _____ _____ juice?"
          a color   a fruit

     "Ewwww!" _____ and I exclaimed.
                    the first friend

     "What's wrong with _____
                                   the same kind of food

salad?" _____ said angrily.
            the second friend

     "Nothing," I answered. "It's just that I hate

_____ salad!"
     the same kind of food

Have you read all about Freddy?

Freddy will do anything to lose a tooth fast—even if it means getting in trouble with Mom!

Now that Freddy's found the best show-and-tell ever, how will he sneak his secret into school?

It's report time again, and Freddy's nocturnal research turns up some unexpected results!

Will Freddy find a special skill in time for the big event?